Evvy – Be inspired
to do great things!
♡ Lisa Camp

To Bryan, my husband, who sees me, and often believes in my dreams before I do.

To my children, Griffin and Sydney Faith. Never doubt that the smallest gesture can make the biggest impact.

MASCOT KIDS!
an imprint of Amplify Publishing Group

www.mascotbooks.com

The Smartest Little Worker Ant

©2023 Lisa Camp. All Rights Reserved. No part of this publication may be reproduced, stored in a retrieval system or transmitted in any form by any means electronic, mechanical, or photocopying, recording or otherwise without the permission of the author.

For more information, please contact:
Mascot Kids, an imprint of Amplify Publishing Group
620 Herndon Parkway, Suite 320
Herndon, VA 20170
info@mascotbooks.com

Library of Congress Control Number: 2022919934

CPSIA Code: PRKF1122A

ISBN-13: 978-1-63755-399-2

Printed in China

Out in the grass of a yard down the street,
is the nicest clan of ants that you'll ever meet.

Piled above the green shards of the cool, shiny grass,
a tower of dirt peeks at all who should pass.
And in that most incredible home
is a family of ants. All are welcome, bar none.

Now it's known far and wide,
wide and far, cross the yard:
the ants are good workers,
they work very hard.
Lifting and sifting huge
grains of dirt
and helping each other so
no one gets hurt.

What's this we see in the shade of a stump?
But a young little ant on a rock . . . on his rump.
He mutters and giggles and laughs to himself,
"I'm the coolest ant here and I need not help.
I am so small and my muscles so few.
My help does not matter, what can I do?
There are so many ants who work hard each day.
Who will take notice if I just go play?"

So off he wanders from family and friends, past mushrooms and weeds and dandelions.

"Work, work, work...
just to build a house of dirt!
My family is silly," he sings as he laughs.
"They work and they strain, yet they get nothing back!

"I want something more; I want to be free.
To sing and to play whenever I please.
Why, oh why would you sweat and toil
just to relocate a whole bunch of soil?
They will not miss me, they won't even know
if my work is not done. It won't even show."

In the midst of his song, there booms such a thunder.
The little ant scatters to a leaf and climbs under.
When the thunder is finished, it opens the sky,
and the rain starts to fall as the heavens do cry.

Now remember the size of a teardrop of rain
and the size of an ant . . .
well, they're just not the same!

"I'll drown!" shrieks the ant as he rushes up a stalk
of grass and scurries up to the top.
Holding on dearly, he peers cross the yard
at the pile of dirt that is getting hit hard.
He sees friends and neighbors, he sees family too,
rushing around with no clue what to do.

And then it hits him, he knows what is right, watching them struggle with all of their might. "They DO need my help! How could I have known? They're working so hard to protect MY home!"

He leaps so bravely from the tall shard of grass
and hurries back to the pile to help out with the rest.
By the time it is over, the dirt pile is gone,
and the ants just all sit there with sad faces on.

But then something happens to get his attention,
with no mutter or phrase or word ever mentioned.
All the ants stand up with not so much as a sound,
and begin to pick grains of dirt from the ground.

One by one, grain by grain, they gather and pile,
and march in a line as long as an ant mile.
Putting each little piece on top of the next
'til a new house is standing, looking its best.

And the smartest little ant in the yard that day
was the one who would say,
"No matter how little, no matter how small,
you must do your part to help one—to help all."

The lesson we've learned is simple at best:
No matter the size of yourself or your test,
if each person does but only their share,
the work will get done without ever a care.

ABOUT THE AUTHOR

Lisa Camp is a wife, mother, teacher, and lover of all creatures, great and small. She grew up in Abilene, Texas, and has taught secondary art in public schools for the last twenty-three years. The kids Lisa has taught come up with many questions, fun ideas, and quirky observations, providing an abundance of material to write about! With her children's book, *The Smartest Little Worker Ant*, Lisa hopes to combine her love for animals and her desire to tell stories that teach kids good moral lessons.